ACROSS THE FRONTIER

Andersen Young Readers' Library

Christine Pullein-Thompson

ACROSS THE FRONTIER

Illustrated by Laszlo Acs

Andersen Press · London

First published in 1990 by
Andersen Press Limited,
20 Vauxhall Bridge Road, London SW1

British Library Cataloguing in Publication Data
Pullein-Thompson, Christine
Across the frontier.
I. Title II. Acs, Laszlo
823'.914[J]

ISBN 0-86264-298-1

Typesetting by Print Origination (NW) Limited, Formby, Liverpool
Printed and bound in Great Britain by Courier International Limited,
Tiptree, Essex

Contents

1
They Come

He drove the cows and the young bull calf along the sandy road. It was still hot and there was dust everywhere and plums hanging over-ripe on trees. Children were driving geese home along the road in front of him. In the distance oxen were pulling a cart laden with wood. He strained his eyes ahead along the road, but there was nothing else. They haven't come, he thought; they said today, but they haven't come.

His grandmother was sitting outside the house. Her dark hair had turned grey; she had small dark eyes, smaller and darker than his own.

'They haven't come,' he said.

The postman was coming along the road now in his horse and cart, but he did not stop, just flourished his whip and went on in a cloud of dust.

'They can still come,' his grandmother said. 'I'll milk the cow, Ion. You fetch the geese in.'

It was months since they had written. He had read the letter. The envelope was stamped with the Queen of England's head. It was a short letter, saying only that they were coming after all

these years; all of them, his father's brother and his family. '*We will come in a Camper*,' the letter said, '*so don't worry about beds*.' And neither he nor his grandmother knew what a Camper was . . . . He went through the big yard gates to fetch the geese. They were waiting, their necks stretched out, their throats quaking silently. The gander led the way in, looking important, as though he alone knew the path to bed.

Ion looked up the road again, but there were only children bringing oxen home and a man leading a bicycle, his clothes white from the cement mines over the hill. He fetched buckets from the house, which had three rooms and a verandah in front, and took them to the pump and waited to fill them.

'They haven't come then,' said an old man.

'It's a long way,' replied a woman who wore a head-scarf as all the women did, except when they were inside their own houses.

Everyone knew they were coming, everyone was watching.

'I remember Fanel as a boy,' said the old man. 'A proper devil.'

'Pity about Lucian,' said someone else. 'They were as thick as thieves when they were children.'

'They will meet in heaven,' replied an old woman and crossed herself.

Lucian was his father, who had been taken away with his mother by the soldiers; or was it the police? No one seemed sure, though they went to the nearby town and never came back. People said that they had hidden money for a friend, or written letters to a prisoner. No one really knew, and Ion could not remember them at all.

It was his turn at the pump now. The sun was

going down behind the vineyards like a ball of fire. He looked down the road again, which was rutted by the Co-operative Farm's tractors, and there was no one there, nothing but a small dog scratching himself. He carried the buckets home. 'They aren't coming,' he said. 'They must have changed their minds. It's a long time since we had the letter.'

His grandmother had finished milking. 'They will come in their own good time,' she replied. 'Fetch the cows some maize leaves, and then come in to supper.'

She was growing old. He could see it in the way she walked, bent by the weight of a bucket of milk. She had lost three teeth since the spring. She was much slower than she had been last year. It made him sad. I shall stay here forever until she's dead, he thought. I'll look after her.

The cows wrapped their wet tongues round the stalks and leaves of the maize which he threw down in front of them. They swished their tails and settled down to eat. Some children were driving sheep along the road outside, a little boy toddling behind them without pants. There was the sound of crickets and a baby crying and nothing else.

When he went inside supper was ready - two dishes of mush made from maize flour, with eggs on top and goat cheese.

'They are never going to come. I feel it in my bones,' he said sitting down at the table. A rug decorated the wall. The table was covered by a cloth made from flax they had gathered themselves, soaked in stagnant water, beaten and woven.

'I've looked forward to them coming the whole summer,' he said. 'And now they haven't come.'

'They said the end of August. It is only the last day today,' his grandmother replied. 'They may have had trouble at the frontier, who knows?'

'Who knows anything?' he asked. 'People can disappear without a trace.'

'Not now; it's changed. Not any more.'

He felt sick with disappointment. She is wrong. Nothing ever changes, he thought bitterly. It's the same year after year - the spring, the long, hot summer, the grapes and the plum brandy, the new year, the spring again. Chicks and calves . . . the same people, the same walk to school, the same long holidays.

There was electricity, but no tap in the house. The rooms were heated by two stoves fed with wood. His legs were covered with mosquito bites; his hands were calloused from carrying buckets backwards and forwards to the pump. But without him his grandmother would never survive; he could see that now. A month ago she had started to crochet. She had made his uncle a whole set of table mats already, while he had made baskets from young willows cut from over the hill. The baskets were in a corner of the room where he slept, waiting like he had waited, almost the whole summer.

'He was bigger than your father,' his grandmother said. 'Not taller, but bigger made. People said he was a fine boy.' She was talking about the uncle he had never seen. Her eyes were full of tears while outside dusk had come. He left the table and stood on the verandah outside, thinking, it's the first of September tomorrow, the holidays are nearly over.

And then he heard someone shouting, 'Ion, they've come. They're coming now.' People rushed to their gates, while he called, 'They're coming, Grandma.'

Another minute and he was running down the road shouting and waving, forgetting that he had no shoes on, that his shirt missed two buttons, that he was supposed to be wearing his best white shirt, his crisp brown shorts and patent leather shoes. A dog rushed at him barking. He hurled a stone towards it and all the time he could see the Camper coming closer. His uncle drove it carefully, avoiding the ruts. There were children's

heads hanging out of the windows. One shouted, 'Can't we get out, Daddy? Can't we run?' But Ion knew no English. He could only wave and stare at his father's brother whom he had never seen before. A crowd of children stood watching from beside the pump. Grandmother was outside now in the road, her face soaked with tears.

'My son, my son,' she called. 'Let me see you.

It's been a long time.'

Uncle Fanel was tall, with hair receding from his forehead and even in the dusk his face was pale compared with Ion's.

Everyone was looking at the Camper now. They felt it and stroked it and touched the wipers and smiled. The children inside tumbled out.

'Well, here we are,' said Fanel. 'After twenty-five years. What do you think of it, Marian?'

She was his wife, who stood uncertainly in the dusk, wearing trousers and checked shirt and sandals.

'It's fabulous,' she said at last, but she spoke in English so neither Ion nor his grandmother understood.

'Open the yard gate, Ion,' his grandmother said. 'Let them bring the car in.'

His English cousins were wearing jeans, and shirts with all their buttons on and leather sandals. Ion felt shabby as he struggled with the gate, and jealous too because they had a father and mother and a Camper. They have everything, he thought. They are the lucky ones. I would like Uncle Fanel for a father, though I'm not sure about the mother.

'Shut the gate, Ion,' shouted Grandma. 'And latch it well.'

They were going inside now, laughing and talking, while he pushed the heavy gates shut and wiped his face with the back of his hand, which left a dirty mark. The yard dogs were yapping wildly and leaping in a frenzy of excitement at the end of their chains.

Inside the house Uncle Fanel was saying, 'It hasn't changed. It's just the same. But I miss Lucian.' The children were sitting on Ion's bed talking to one another in English. They looked at the carpets and shuttered windows and asked, 'Where did you sleep, Daddy, when you were little?'

Ion stood in the doorway watching his grandmother, who had changed completely. She fetched bottles of wine from the cellar, running up and down steps like a girl.

'We must celebrate,' she said, stopping to kiss her grandchildren each in turn on both cheeks. 'Drink, please drink, all of you.'

2
'We Want to Watch'

Donald was the eldest child. Tall and lean with dark hair, everyone called him Don. Next came Sandra, who was like her mother with brown hair and blue eyes; she laughed a lot and she had a ridiculously small nose which turned up at the end. Marcus was fair with brown eyes. 'A Russian,' Grandma called him laughing, hugging him round the shoulders before she picked up the youngest of them all, four-year-old Rosie, who had cheeks the colour of apples.

'What a family!' Grandma said to Uncle Fanel. 'But why the English names? Only Marcus has a nice name.'

'They are English,' replied Uncle Fanel, 'because they were born there.'

'What about something to eat?' asked Grandma a moment later. But they had eaten. They wanted nothing besides biscuits from the Camper.

'We will kill five chickens tomorrow,' Grandma said. 'We will have a feast and Ion will take you up to the vineyard.'

Ion nodded from his corner. He felt very tired now. Grandma started to discuss beds. 'You can have Ion's bed. He can sleep in the barn,' she said.

'That wouldn't be fair,' replied Uncle Fanel.

'Go on with you. When was life fair? He's slept there before,' cried Grandma, half-drunk with wine and plum brandy.

Outside all the dogs of the village were barking. It was the same every night. They barked for an hour when it was dark; then again at sunrise. The sky was still light where the sun had gone down. The earth was warm under Ion's bare feet. He wished he could talk English as he walked to the barn. Inside the cows were lying down in their stalls. He climbed onto a pile of hay. He could see the sky through the cracks in the roof. It was a dark, velvety sky. He could hear mosquitoes buzzing overhead. He lay on the hay and scratched. They are so rich, he thought. They have everything.

Morning came with the crowing of cocks and the dogs' barking. The house was still in darkness. The yard dogs had been out all night and were waiting to be let in. He could hear a child already up, driving goats along the road outside. He had slept in his clothes so there was no need to dress. He went outside and washed quickly under the pump. I wonder if they can milk, he thought. His grandmother was up now. He could see the light

in her window. She opened the back door to call softly, 'Ssh, don't make a noise. They are still asleep.' Her hair hung in a plait down her back. Presently she would wind it round her head and secure it with pins before putting on a head-scarf.

Or kill a chicken, he thought, or know the difference between the grapes.

'Your hair is full of hay. Come inside and brush it,' Grandma called.

More people were passing outside now, padding through the dust in bare feet. They stopped to look at the Camper. They greeted him, saying, 'They came then. What a lovely car!'

He brushed his hair, wishing he was taller, that

his arms were straighter, that he was different altogether.

'You mustn't be miserable,' Grandma said, reading his thoughts. 'You are all right as you are. They are different because they are English.'

'Only half,' he answered, going outside with a bucket to milk the cows.

There was a radio on across the road, sending opera songs into the clear, hot, morning air. The few people who had radios kept them full on, so that their neighbours would benefit too. He milked the old cow before he went inside for breakfast. The English children were getting up. The three eldest appeared sleepy-eyed from the Camper. Rosie had slept with her parents in Ion's bed. She kept crying and asking for things, while Don said, 'Hot, very hot,' and pointed to the sky and laughed. Sandra pretended to wipe sweat from her face. Then she looked at the young chickens and said, 'Pretty, very pretty,' in Ion's language.

He picked one up and said, 'Yes, me, this . . . ' and pretended to cut its head off. But Sandra didn't laugh. She hid her face and shouted, 'No, please no,' and then she said, 'You cruel, very cruel.'

He pretended that he was eating the chicken, because he thought she did not understand. 'You too,' he said. 'You eat it, too, soon.'

Inside Uncle Fanel was saying to Grandma, 'It is different in England. They have never seen anything killed. Marian buys them trussed up ready for the oven, from the supermarket. They are not like chickens at all.'

'But how do they taste?' Grandma asked, licking her lips.

'Like string,' replied Uncle Fanel laughing. 'I've been looking forward to young chicken all the way here.'

So they eat chicken, Ion thought. But how can one eat chicken without killing it? Someone must kill it. Sandra would not look at him, but Don was laughing. Perhaps he too can kill a chicken, decided Ion.

Aunt Marian fetched food from the Camper - cornflakes and sugar, bread and marmalade. 'The butter didn't last,' she said. Grandma found them bowls. It was hot already.

'I've been out and I've eaten nine plums, five pears and eleven apples,' said Marcus appearing. 'The gander tried to chase me, but I shouted at him.'

'You are not to go out alone,' Grandma cried, looking at him. 'Only with Ion.'

Marcus only knew English. He smiled and asked his father what Grandma was saying. But Ion knew. He said, 'You come with me,' and took his arm.

'You should have taught them our language,' Grandma said.

'I'm teaching them now,' smiled Uncle Fanel.

Ion had to take the cows to pasture. The English children came too, except for Rosie who

stayed behind playing with plastic English toys in the dusty yard.

Ion picked pears and gave them to the children. He pulled down green walnuts and cut them open and said, 'Eat, eat please.' He was already picking up some English. Presently he found that Sandra and Don were learning French like himself; so that was a third language they could use.

Geese were cropping the roadside grass; there was a constant passing of oxen and carts and once the schoolmaster, Ion's father's cousin, passed, with his grey horse and cart. The English children took off their shoes to walk barefoot like Ion. They had reached the open common where all the villagers grazed their animals. There were other children there already. A boy sat on a boulder watching pigs root for nuts. Two girls in short dresses were watching goats, two other girls lay in the grass watching three sheep. A man passed them carrying wood on his back. They could see a railway line in the distance, a river and then nothing but hills as far as the eye could see.

The English children had brought toy guns, so they played a shooting game, dodging behind bushes and boulders. When it was too hot to run any more Ion took the cows and the little bull calf home along the dusty road, stopping to water them at the well, where he drew the water up in a bucket and tipped it into a trough made from a tree trunk. The heat made the English children dizzy. Their white skin was turning red. Everyone turned to look at them. 'There are the English children,' they said.

But they are not really English, Ion thought, only half, the other half belongs here in this village where their father grew up. But they looked like foreigners and so did Uncle Fanel, who Grandma said had changed beyond all recognition, whatever that might mean.

The cows were easy to drive but the calf ran all ways.

'Do you have a cow?' asked Ion pointing.

They shook their heads. 'Only a dog,' replied Don, barking loudly.

'And a cat,' added Sandra miaowing.

'And my mice,' cried Marcus squeaking.

Ion liked them; they made the house seem full of fun and laughter. He was never bored with them.

3
Ion Makes up his Mind

The days passed, hot, sunlit days. The English children grew brown. Aunt Marian dressed Ion's mosquito bites. She gave him ointment which kept the mosquitoes away. He slept with the two boys in the Camper now and ate cereals for breakfast and baked beans for supper. The house was full of laughter. He began to wish that they were staying for ever. It will be quiet and empty when they're gone, he thought to himself over and over again. People came to see them, half-forgotten relations who always said, 'What a pity Lucian isn't here, but how well his son is, and what a good boy.'

Uncle Fanel gave him money for fetching water from the pump and for bringing them grapes from the vineyard over the hill. It was a long walk there, uphill all the way along a path which wound between bushes where lizards hid. Sometimes he would see a tortoise moving slowly in front. But it meant nothing to him. He could think of nothing but England now; of roads full of cars and shops full of toys and television in all the houses. The English children had made it sound like fairyland.

He started to complain about having to drive the cows to pasture. 'Other children don't have to do it,' he told his grandmother. 'Other children have bikes and lots of toys and they never work except at school.'

'It will come to that here too,' replied his grandmother, shaking her head, 'but not in my lifetime.'

Sandra did not wish to leave. 'Not yet, not for a bit longer,' she kept saying. Don helped him fetch water from the pump. Marcus complained about the dogs being chained up. 'It's cruel,' he said. 'How would you like to be chained up hour after hour?' He pretended not to understand. They were peculiar over animals. They treated them as though they were people. They thought they had feelings. Ion thought of them like trees; something which was born and grew and then died; something which did not feel or think, which just existed.

Uncle Fanel took them all out in the Camper. They had a picnic at the side of the road and Rosie was stung by a bee and she cried for hours. There were geese by the roadside and a granny dressed in black watching over them.

'Only three more days,' said Uncle Fanel.

'It has been a wonderful holiday,' replied Aunt Marian, rocking Rosie in her arms.

'I shall pack you some food for the journey and you must take some wine and plum brandy,' said Grandma.

It was too hot to move; one just existed until the evening came. Oxen were pulling wagons loaded with tubs of fermenting plums when they returned to the village. It was plum brandy time already.

'Our plums go tomorrow at five, it's our turn for the vats. Be up early tomorrow, Ion. The men will be coming to help,' said Grandma. 'You'll have to be there all day.'

For the first time in his life he didn't want to be there looking after the wagon and the cows, sitting round the wood fire, tasting the brandy, eating young goat roasted over a wood fire. 'Do I have to go?' he asked.

'Of course. Who else is there?' Grandma asked. 'You've always gone. You are expected.'

'I'll sleep in the barn,' he said. 'I wake easier there.'

They were home now. Uncle Fanel parked the Camper. 'Come inside, I want to talk to you,' he said, putting one arm round Ion's shoulder. 'I have a suggestion to make. It's been in my mind a long time.'

They sat in the front room; the blinds were down. It was cool and silent. 'Sit beside me,' said

Uncle Fanel. He smelt of after-shave lotion. He was soft, like someone who doesn't walk much.

'We wondered whether you would like to come back with us. We have made some sort of arrangements. We think we can get you out,' he said.

Ion thought he was dreaming. He said, 'Please say that again,' and his head seemed to be whirling round and round with a mass of thoughts all trying to get in, while Uncle Fanel repeated himself. Ion imagined England . . . the cars, the shops, the pies you bought ready-made, fish and chips, the underground trains. Don had described them all.

'For ever? Do you mean for ever?' he asked.

Uncle Fanel nodded. 'You could never come back,' he said. 'It would be too risky.'

'What about Grandma?'

'She must stay. She can manage. It is you we must think of. You've got years and years in front of you.'

He thought of Grandma fetching water from the pump, waking up alone in the house, driving the cows to pasture, doing the jobs he did now, alone, always alone.

He said, 'I don't know.'

'Take your time,' replied Uncle Fanel sitting with his hands in his lap. 'But if I were you I should say yes. I left here when I was seventeen and I've never regretted it.'

London, Ion thought. There's everything in London . . . .And when I'm grown up I can have a sports car, a new house, everything. I'll never have to watch the cows again. Grandma, he thought, she's looked after me all these years, she's brought me up. I meant to look after her for ever.

'Take your time,' repeated Uncle Fanel, standing up. 'Think about it. I'm sure you will say yes in the end. We won't forget Grandma. We'll send her parcels and write; you can write every week. She'll want you to go. I know she will.'

'Have you asked him?' asked Don coming into the room. 'Is he coming?'

'He hasn't decided.'

'You can have my bike. It's just your size, and it's nearly new,' Don said. 'And we've got a big garden and there's a cinema just down the road. It's a super place.'

Ion saw himself on a new bike, wearing English clothes. He looked at his mosquito-bitten legs and bare feet, and still he couldn't decide.

'It's Grandma. I'm thinking of Grandma,' he said in his own tongue.

There seemed no air in the room. He felt as though he was suffocating. He wished there was someone who would simply say, Do this or Do that. He rushed outside and drove the cows along the dusty road. He wanted to be alone. The sun was going down below the hills. Everything was beautiful. It was as it had been for hundreds of years; nothing changed. Everyone knew him. It was home. I don't know what to say, he thought with a sense of panic. They may grow tired of me in England. I may quarrel with Don . . . and then there's Grandma. Ion looked at the rolling hills and knew he loved them. He loved every twist in the path to the vineyard too; and the two cows with their large, placid eyes. He picked a plum and ate it. He sat on the wiry grass and watched them graze. Everything was quiet.

Ion stayed there a long time. When he started for home he had made up his mind. He had hardened his heart against Grandma. Like Uncle Fanel said, she was old. She had not long to live. But he had his whole life - he was going. He said goodbye to everything as he went back, to the hill where his grandfather was buried, to the little valley where he had gathered willow for the baskets, to the single-storey houses with their verandahs in front, to the well where he had drawn water so often for the animals, to the heat and the mosquitoes, and to the simple white school where he

had studied.

'I'm going,' he said standing in the kitchen while his grandmother laid the long trestle table for dinner outside in the yard. She shrugged her shoulders and said nothing, whereas Sandra threw her arms round his neck and screamed, 'He's coming with us, Daddy, he's coming.'

And Uncle Fanel slapped him on his back. 'You won't regret it,' he promised. 'This country is no

place for an enterprising young man like you.'

'He'll have to share Marcus's room,' said Aunt Marian thoughtfully, 'and he'll need a mass of new clothes.'

They ate a feast that night and toasted Ion again and again until he felt quite giddy, and the air was full of the buzz of insects and the slow tread of oxen.

'We leave in two days,' said Uncle Fanel. 'We

brought two passports. You are on the second. You must not open your mouth at the border. We will dress you in English clothes and scrub your face till it shines pink. You must remember that from now on, you are our child.'

Grandma didn't look at him. What was she thinking? He would never know. 'Supposing they speak to me?' asked Ion.

'I will answer, or the children will. We'll all start talking at once. You must not worry. Everything is fixed. We don't even need a picture of you. The passport is stamped as though you entered with us. You understand, don't you?'

He nodded slowly. He was afraid now. It was bad enough leaving, but to leave illegally, that was worse. 'If they find out they will start shooting,' he said in his own tongue. 'They always do.'

'Don't worry, son, it's all arranged. You are our son too now like Don and Marcus. We'll adopt you the minute we get home, won't we, Marian?'

His grandmother would not let them help wash the dishes; but Ion dried for her, looking at her constantly until at last she felt obliged to ask, 'Well, what is it? Why do you look at me so often?'

'To see if you mind my going.'

'Of course I mind. It is like losing another

son,' she replied. 'The last one. But I cannot stand in your way. If life is better there, you must go. And don't worry, I shall manage. I am still strong.' But for how much longer? he wondered.

'I have managed before,' she said. 'And I shall manage again. Remember you must be up at four to help with the brandy. Your uncle will want to take some with him, and some of last year's wine too, and chicken to eat on the journey. We shall be very busy. And then we must pack for you. I have a keepsake for you . . . something you must treasure all your life.'

'What, what is it?' Ion cried.

'You will know before you go,' she replied, tipping the dirty washing-up water into the yard. 'And that is soon enough.'

4

'You Must Smell English'

It was dark when Ion rose the next morning from his bed of hay and hurried outside to harness the two cows which would pull the two stills of fermenting plums down to the place where they would be distilled into brandy. It would take all day. Presently his great-uncle came and a peasant called Vasile and they loaded the vats onto the cart without saying much and, as they worked, dawn came with a strip of light in the east which widened slowly into another day. And Ion thought, this is the last time. He walked in front and the two men followed behind watching the vats. He had brought a bucket so that he could milk the cows. Someone called, 'Good luck with your brandy, Ion. You are a good boy. God be with you.'

They spent the day there, blackened by the smoke from the fire, tasting the brandy when at last it was distilled, feeling its fire run through them. Someone brought a kid and they roasted it there on a wood fire. There were twelve of them now and they drank red wine made from the grapes on the hill. And Uncle Fanel and Aunt

Marian and the children came in the Camper with Grandma and the men took off their caps to them and bowed. And Ion wondered, will they treat me like that if I come back? Will I be someone special to be admired? They tasted the brandy and the smoke-roast kid and Uncle Fanel smacked his lips and passed compliments. And slowly the dripping brandy stopped dripping and someone said, 'That's the lot.' They loaded the brandy onto the cart in barrels and Ion went back along the road for the last time, biting his lips to stop himself crying, with his face black from the fire and his hard hands red with wine. He said goodbye to his village all over again, before he fetched a bucket of water from the pump so that the English children could wash; and he thought, I shall never feel as they do. I shall never get used to having things, to sitting and playing all day long. And must I really call Uncle Fanel Father and Aunt Marian, Mother? Or worse still, Daddy and Mummy? I would rather call them uncle and aunt, because half of me will always belong here.

Uncle Fanel stood watching him and seemed to read his thoughts, for he smiled at Ion and said, 'You will forget. Soon all this will seem just like a dream. In a year you will feel completely English, I promise, though it will take a little longer to learn the language fluently.'

Ion stayed very close to Grandma that evening. He half hoped she would say, 'Don't go.' But her old face told him nothing, and she did not speak about him leaving except to make arrangements for the journey, to pack great baskets of food into the Camper, and send him in the dusk to the vineyard to fetch still more grapes. His legs would hardly carry him there and his arms ached, but the view from the hill seemed more beautiful than ever before, with lights twinkling in the distance and the voices of children speaking in his own language, which soon he wouldn't need any more.

And what if they shoot at me at the border? he thought, going down the hill homewards. Will they take me to prison? But suddenly that didn't matter either for his parents might be still alive, working their lives away in a concentration camp. He might get word of them. No, that did not matter at all. There was a crowd of peasants waiting at the gate. They had brought presents. His best friend had carved him a cow from a piece of wood; Nina, a dark-haired girl, had worked him a tablecloth. A tall peasant who had known his father had brought him a pen. 'Good luck,' he said. 'We will miss you.'

They had brought presents too for the English children. They were so poor, yet they were always giving presents. There were many farewells said that night, kisses and embraces, good wishes and promises. Then there was Grandma's present, a locket with a strand of his mother's hair inside and the photograph of his parents which had stood for so long on the table by her bed. 'It is yours now. Treasure it,' she said. 'You may never see them again, but at least you will know them as they were on their wedding day.'

He looked at his moustached father, stiff and formal in his best suit, and at his mother in her wedding dress. So they had had a church wedding, he thought. Not many people did that nowadays. They did not believe in God. The church stood empty on the hill. Goats and young calves were tethered in the churchyard, even sometimes a pig.

He said, 'Thank you, Grandma,' and kissed her cheek, which was parched like leather.

'God be with you,' she replied. She had not lost her faith. She still prayed sometimes, kneeling old and withered like fruit which has been kept too long, in her black dress and shawl.

'I will write, Grandma, I promise. I will send you clothes - skirts, warm stockings and beautiful shoes.'

'And what will I do with them? I am too old for change. I am happy enough as I am,' she replied.

The English children did not wish to leave. 'It's so lovely here,' Marcus said. 'So peaceful with no cars. And we can play with the chicks and eat plums and grapes all day long. I wish I could stay for ever.'

'But . . . ' began Ion in his own tongue, but stopped because he could not put into words what he was thinking - that they had boasted about England, turned it into a sort of fairyland where the streets were paved with gold, and yet now they did not want to go. It did not make sense. And Marcus was actually crying in a corner now. 'We didn't have to be clean and tidy here,' he said. 'We didn't have to bother about the neighbours. I don't want to leave.'

'Don't be silly,' replied his mother. 'You have everything at home.'

Uncle Fancl looked at Ion. 'They don't mean it,' he said. 'They love England. And we'll take you everywhere - to Buckingham Palace where the Queen lives, to the Changing of the Guard, to the Zoo . . . .'

'Thank you,' replied Ion. 'I will like that.'

Ion rose early next day because he wanted to leave everything tidy for his grandmother. He fed and milked the cows. He let out the geese to roam at will. He filled up all the house buckets and jugs with water and took the cows to pasture. Friends were already assembling by the pump to watch him leave. His cousin called bearing honey. The postman brought a letter. Sadly Ion drove the cows back along the sandy road, knowing that it must be almost time to leave. Goodbye road, goodbye pasture, goodbye, goodbye everything, he said to himself and could feel tears pricking behind his eyes.

Uncle Fanel was in the yard loading up the Camper. 'Hurry, Ion,' he called. 'Go and have breakfast and then wash, wash as you've never washed before. You hair too, everything.'

There was water heating on the stove in the kitchen which burnt wood. 'You must wash,' said Grandma, 'but first eat your mush.'

It was hot already, and the stove made it hotter. He sat at the table outside and ate his mush. 'Marian will cut his hair the English way,' called Uncle Fanel. 'She was a hairdresser when I married her.'

Some English clothes were laid out ready for him, a T-shirt, jeans, socks and brown leather sandals. His grandmother filled the tin bath she used for washing clothes with water. 'Wash,' she said. 'Here is some soap.' It was English soap, not like the soap they made themselves in the village. It smelt of flowers.

'You must smell English too,' she said.

'Let me cut his hair first. I can't cut it wet,' cried Aunt Marian. She cut swiftly and as he watched locks of his dark hair falling, it was like losing part of himself, the part which belonged to his own country.

'Hurry now,' cried Grandma when the cutting was finished. 'Into the tub with you, and scrub yourself, you must look pink, not brown.'

They left him to wash himself and now the fire was dying down and he could look round the kitchen and try to engrave its appearance on his mind for ever.

He scrubbed himself, but when he stepped out of the water and looked at himself in a mirror he was still brown. He stepped back and scrubbed himself again and again until Uncle Fanel called through the door, 'Not ready yet? Hurry, Ion. It is gone ten o'clock. We should be on the road by now.'

He dried himself and put on the English clothes, buckling the sandals carefully, tucking in the shirt. Grandma came in then. 'Ready?' she asked. 'You look all right. You will do.' She took his face in her hands and kissed him. 'Good luck,' she said.

The Camper was loaded, his luggage stacked with the others. A crowd waited outside to watch him go. He walked uneasily in the sandals, which were too large. He didn't look at his grandmother again, because if he had he would have cried. He looked at the buildings instead, where he had spent so many hours tending the animals. He waved to the people waiting and cried, 'I'll come back and see you when I'm rich. I'll have a big car.' And they laughed, calling, 'Remember us at Christmas.'

Grandma stood at the gate watching him go and someone called, 'Don't worry, we'll look after her.' But he thought she looked very old and lonely standing there, old and betrayed.

'You have to live your own life,' said Uncle Fanel putting a hand on his knee. 'They will look after her in the village.'

'You look English already,' said Aunt Marian, but she did not touch him. He had noticed that she hardly ever touched anyone, whereas the people in the village were for ever kissing hands and cheeks, embracing old friends, hugging children.

'We will spend tonight in a hotel,' said Uncle Fanel. 'We'll eat in our room. Then you need not pretend to be English. Have you stayed in a hotel before?'

Ion shook his head while his cousins laughed. 'Haven't you seen the sea either?' they cried. He shook his head again. He had never been further than twenty miles from the village, which was something they would never understand; yet in his own way he had been quite happy.

'Try and keep your arms straight,' said Aunt Marian presently. 'They are bent from carrying so many buckets. You walk like a labourer and it shows.' She said it in English so he only half understood. He looked at his arms and wondered what was wrong with them. She leaned over from the front seat and tried to make them straight.

'Leave him alone. He's all right,' said Uncle Fanel. 'He's a good boy.'

They had reached new country now, country which he had never seen before, fruit farms and a great river. He longed to take off his shoes, to roam across the hills and cool his feet in the river. They picnicked by a spring. The day was unbearably hot now and the car wheels sent up great clouds of dust as they drove.

Aunt Marian said, 'Try to walk as though you always wear shoes, Ion, and swing your arms and relax; you look on edge. The customs men will be sure to smell a rat.'

'Leave the boy alone,' said Uncle Fanel. 'You are one of us now; you have brothers and sisters. You must call us Mother and Father.'

Ion nodded. The English children were complaining of the heat now. 'Isn't there any shade anywhere?' cried Marcus.

Five minutes later they were moving on. 'Don't talk in the hotel,' said Uncle Fanel. 'You mustn't be noticed. You understand?'

Ion nodded. There was a lump rising in his throat. He was afraid he would never change in time. He would still walk like a peasant when he reached the frontier; his arms would give him away; he would exclaim about something in his own tongue and they would all be arrested and marched away by the soldiers.

They could see the town now where they were to spend the evening. It was a squat town lying in a valley on the banks of a great river. On all sides there were vineyards, and state farms with new white buildings and machines which threshed the corn and tractors which ploughed quicker than the oxen. He had never been so far from home before.

'We won't stay at the tourist hotel,' said Uncle Fanel. 'It'll be full of secret service men watching us. We will stay somewhere simple.'

'With a bathroom,' said Aunt Marian. 'I want a bath.'

Ion had never seen a bathroom.

They found a hotel in the centre of the town. They parked outside. A boy not much older than Ion carried their cases inside. Uncle Fanel asked for a room with a bath. There was a marble floor in the hall and marble stairs, and ferns in pots. Ion thought it a very grand place. But Aunt Marian described it as old-fashioned.

There were two adjoining rooms with three beds in each. One could open the windows and look down into the street.

'It is a very grand room,' exclaimed Ion in spite of himself. 'Is your house as smart as this?'

Uncle Fanel translated his words into English and they all laughed.

'It's modern with big windows. We have television and a garden. It's quite different I assure you,' laughed Aunt Marian. 'And we don't wash our clothes by lighting a fire in the back yard and hanging a pot over it like your grandmother. We have a machine which does the washing.' She made a noise like a machine and pretended to wash the clothes. 'It is much easier,' she said, still laughing.

The sun was going down. It turned the roofs of the town red. The pavements outside were cool at last. The shops were still open. They would not shut for hours yet.

'Only five more miles to the frontier,' said Uncle Fanel stretching. 'Who wants to come outside and buy some food? No, not you, Ion. You must lie low till we reach the West.'

'Will I be able to go out alone in England?' Ion asked.

Uncle Fanel laughed. 'Of course,' he cried. 'In England you will be free.'

Free! thought Ion looking at the sandals he was wearing. Had he not always been free to roam where he would when he was not at school or attending the animals? He had roamed for miles with his friends, as far as the cement factory, returning home white with dust like the workers. He had spent long happy hours lying under the fruit trees. No one had ever remarked on his arms, or tried to change the colour of his sunburned skin or dressed him in foreign clothes. Uncle Fanel was watching him. He had grown up as Ion had in the village. He understood.

'No one is arrested and kept in England without a fair trial, Ion,' he said gently. 'They don't simply disappear in the night, and they are not tortured.'

Tortured! How often he had imagined his parents tortured. His mother so young and beautiful in her wedding photograph. Had they tortured her? He could never be like the English children. They were so carefree. They had never spent a whole day alone watching over a vineyard of grapes as he had done summer after summer, sitting in the watch tower built for the purpose. They couldn't milk a cow, nor kill to eat. They were like artificial flowers.

'I'm coming with you, Daddy,' Rosie was screaming now.

'So am I,' shouted Marcus and Don together.

'You can't leave me behind,' cried Sandra.

'I don't mind staying here alone,' said Ion to his uncle. 'I can practise my English. I am not afraid.'

'You want to go without us, so that you can drink alone in the hotel opposite,' said Aunt Marian. 'How can you be so mean?'

'We will all go,' said Uncle Fanel in a resigned voice. 'Yes, you too, Ion. We can't leave you alone; it would seem odd. Get ready. I will go ahead and buy some food.'

His grandmother had never been inside a bar, but Aunt Marian seemed quite content in her trouser suit sipping a drink and commenting on the other people dotted about at odd tables.

The waiters were smart and quick. They didn't keep the customers waiting. They wanted to please the tourists, so that they would come again. If only I could go away and come back, thought Ion. It would not be such a decision then. It's the finality of it all which is so frightening. The thought that I may never see my village again. The place that I love more than anywhere else on earth. And that I shall certainly never see Grandma again, only the place where she is buried. A band was playing sad gypsy music.

The streets were heavy with dusk, the end of a summer. It was like his mood. It was as though the whole town was saying goodbye to something too, to the end of a summer.

5
The Frontier

Ion hardly slept that night. He shared a double bed with Don. Darkness came; but there were still footsteps going up and down the streets which made Ion think of soldiers coming in the night. The street lamps cast a glow on the carpet which made him think of searchlights watching the frontier, searching for escaping people. My country is like a prison, he thought, but I still love it. Don slept soundly, one arm dangling over the side of the bed. Ion was accustomed to a straw-filled mattress. The hotel bed felt soft though Aunt Marian had complained about hers, which was the same, saying, 'Haven't they heard of interior springs in this country? I shan't sleep a wink, Fanel.' But now Ion could hear her even breathing coming from the next room. Then someone tried his bedroom door and he sat up, holding his breath, trying not to breathe.

It's the soldiers coming for me, he thought. They are going to take me away. He waited for a voice to call, 'Open up.' And Grandma will never know, he thought. She will die never knowing. She'll think I'm in England. But perhaps it's better that way.

But the steps were going away and suddenly Uncle Fanel was beside him saying, 'Don't be scared, my little goat. It is not the soldiers. It is nothing but a drunken man knocking on the wrong door. You must not be afraid.'

'I'm cold, that's all,' said Ion. 'Very, very cold.'

Uncle Fanel fetched his coat and put it on his bed. 'Don't worry,' he said. 'We won't let them get you. Trust us.'

Some time about dawn, when all the cocks would have been crowing in the village, Ion slept. He was awakened by Uncle Fanel bearing a tray with coffee and fresh rolls on it, pale butter and strawberry jam. 'Up, up,' he cried. 'Today is the day. Today we cross the frontier. Today you taste freedom.'

Ion opened his eyes and saw the hotel bedroom and was filled with a homesickness so strong that he felt sick to the depths of his being. He went to the window and looked out, wearing the pyjamas Aunt Marian had given him the night before. He stared down into the street; people were hurrying to work, his people . . . .

The English children, dressed already, were chattering like magpies. 'I shall shoot them with this,' cried Marcus waving a toy pistol.

'I shall bite the head one,' cried Rosie.

'Idiots,' cried Don. 'Do you think they'll be taken in by a toy pistol? Don't you remember the soldiers who were there when we came?'

'Daddy will roar through at ninety miles an hour,' cried Marcus.

'He'll squash them with the wheels,' cried Rosie jumping up and down on one of the beds. 'He'll squash all the shoulders.'

'Soldiers,' corrected Aunt Marian. 'Have some breakfast, Ion. Hurry. You look like an ailing cockerel this morning.'

'I don't want to go to prison,' screamed Rosie.

'Make them be quiet, Marian,' said Uncle Fanel. 'Someone will hear.' He walked up and down the room like an unhappy bear. Ion could hardly eat. He wished he could understand what they were saying. Outside the day was already hot. Grandma would have milked the cows. Now she would be watching them graze under the fruit trees, her hands folded in her lap, and in the field peasants would be gathering in the maize. Aunt Marian was packing. Uncle Fanel piled the empty coffee cups on the tray. Rosie was crying because there was no orange squash.

'I shall be glad to reach civilisation again,' said Aunt Marian snapping a suitcase shut. 'There should be a pile of letters waiting on the mat.'

'We must get Lassie home. Poor Lassie,' said

Sandra. 'I bet the dog hotel was awful. Still, it must be better there than being a dog here, poor things!'

'Ready?' asked Uncle Fanel. 'Now, no more talking, not another word until we are across the frontier.'

'Across the frontier,' cried Marcus. 'It sounds so exciting.'

'What did I say?' roared Uncle Fanel. 'Silence!'

They paid the bill and went out into the bright sunshine. The Camper was waiting at the door, for Uncle Fanel had fetched it from the garage where it had spent the night while Ion was still asleep. Marcus was carrying his toy gun. Rosie had a dolly which Grandma had given her. There were only five miles left now. Ion could have walked it in just over an hour. The countryside was flat, the road straight. Suddenly Ion wanted the five miles to last for ever.

The maize was being carried on wagons pulled by oxen. Such maize! When would he taste its like again? The grapes were being picked for wine. He could see the frontier now. The red and white bar, the no-man's land beyond. The ploughed fields raked smooth so that fresh footsteps would show, the watch towers on stilts with soldiers inside, the searchlights. His heart was pounding against his ribs, his legs felt like jelly. Why did I say yes? he wondered. We'll all go to prison. The English children too. Our hair will be cut off. We will be hung up by our feet. We will have nothing but soup to eat and go barefoot in the snow. Oh God help us!

'Keep calm,' said Uncle Fanel turning to smile. 'This frontier is nothing. Keep your courage for the next one, the one which really leads to freedom.'

He had a vision of his grandfather now. He was a very old man. He took Ion on his knee and spoke: 'You must look after your grandma when I'm gone. You're the only one left. And you must study well at school and never forget this is your country. I am too old to alter things; but you are young, you have your whole life before you. You can make changes. You can wield power and open the prisons, you and your generation. It's up to you,' he had said.

And Ion had forgotten. He had betrayed his grandfather. 'You are the last of our family,' he had said. 'If your parents are dead, as I think they are, you will have this house, everything, but go to the city and study, work hard and anything is possible.' There were tears streaming down Ion's cheeks now. How could he have forgotten? 'I want to get out and kiss the soil,' he said. 'Please, Uncle Fanel.'

'Are you mad? Everyone will see. Wipe your eyes and don't speak,' cried Uncle Fanel.

'Baby,' said Sandra.

'Shut up,' said Marcus, 'or I will shoot you with my pistol.'

Grandfather had died and Grandma had hardly wept. 'It was God's will,' she had said, following the coffin to the hill. And Ion had meant to follow her coffin. It would have been Grandpa's wish. He had wanted him to be a Minister. A Minister in the Assembly. 'We were a great family once,' he had said. 'We owned half the village, before it was taken away from us. Those days will never come back, but you can make life happier for the people.'

They had had horses once, a coach and pair. Ion had followed the coffin in his best suit; but he had never had another suit.

The car was moving on now. Soldiers opened the barrier for them. They talked in English with an accent; they looked in the car and counted the children. Rosie was crying.

'Did you see their guns?' asked Marcus.

'Shut up,' said Don.

'Get out. They want to search the car,' said Uncle Fanel, the skin of his face drawn tight across his cheekbones. They all stepped out onto the asphalt. Aunt Marian lit a cigarette.

The soldiers looked under the carpets in the Camper. They turned the seats upside down; they looked under the cooker and among the cups. They ruffled Marcus's hair and said, 'Russian,' and took his gun and pretended to shoot. Then Uncle Fanel went into an office with them and Aunt Marian said, 'Get back in the car.' And another soldier came and went through the suit-cases.

'They are looking for guns,' said Marcus.

'Shut up,' replied Don.

'I hope Lassie's all right,' exclaimed Sandra.

'They must be looking for something,' argued Marcus.

'Shut up,' replied Don.

The soldier closed the suitcases and said, 'Thank you,' in English and turned towards another car, while Aunt Marian smoked feverishly.

'He was all right,' said Marcus. 'He must be quite intelligent if he can speak English.'

'Shut up,' said Don.

'Daddy's coming,' cried Rosie. 'Look!'

He was carrying the passports, not daring to smile, not yet, not until they were waved through the barrier and were out of no-man's land.

'Come again,' called the soldier opening the second barrier.

'He could still shoot at our tyres,' cried Marcus as they drove through.

'Shut up, you fool,' hissed Don. 'He understands English.'

Uncle Fanel's face relaxed into a smile. 'It worked,' he said. 'So far, so good.'

'There's still the second frontier,' replied Aunt Marian putting out her cigarette.

'Were you scared, Ion?' asked Uncle Fanel in his own language.

'Yes.' He turned to look at the last of his country, but he could only see Grandpa's face and hear him saying, 'You can open the prisons. You're the only one left. You must look after your grandma when I'm gone . . . look after . . . look after . . . .' It was like a record playing over and over again in his head, and here he was leaving, leaving Grandma, his village, his country, everything, not changing anything. It was like running away, yes, running away.

'I'm thirsty,' cried Rosie.

'Shut up,' said Don.

'We'll be stopping in a minute. Be patient,' said Uncle Fanel.

'I hope Lassie's all right,' repeated Sandra.

'We'll be in the West by the evening,' said Aunt Marian.

He wasn't like them. He was not on the same wavelength. He would always have his past to reckon with, his conscience.

'Can't we stop now?' asked Sandra.

'We must get further from the frontier,' replied Uncle Fanel. 'They might send a car after us.'

'I wish they would. Then I could shoot at them with my toy pistol,' cried Marcus.

'Shut up, you fool,' said Don.

They would grow tired of him too. Only Uncle Fanel might understand, because he had left his country too; but he had not made a promise to his grandfather. He had left freely, leaving his brother to inherit the house and the vineyard, which was all they had left. But who would have the vineyard now?

'Ion's crying,' said Rosie.

'I'm not.'

'Well, you look as though you are.'

'Big boys don't cry,' Marcus said.

'Shut up, Rosie.' Don understood. He could feel the tension. He knew that Ion was fighting a mental battle, was trying to come to a decision.

The countryside was flat with white farmsteads and flat fields cut by streams and plain wood artesian wells standing stark and simple on the horizon. The road ran straight on and on into the distance bearing Ion further and further away from his homeland and his ancestors.

'We'll stop here,' said Uncle Fanel presently. 'Then you can stretch your legs.'

The plain was hot. The fields were bare already. In the distance geese were gathered around a stream. Horses stood swishing their tails against the flies - beautiful horses, such horses as Ion had never seen before.

I can't go on, he thought. I can't leave Grandma alone, not after I promised. Don was watching him. 'You didn't want to leave, not really?' he asked.

Ion could not find the right words to answer him. He looked at Don and thought that he was like a young willow, tall and slim, with long slender hands, more English than all the others, except his mother. But he had his father's eyes, as brown as Ion's own.

'We'll move on. It's too hot here,' said Uncle Fanel.

'I don't want to go on,' replied Ion in his own tongue, biting his lips till they bled. 'I want to go back.'

6
Too Old to be Left

'He wants to go back,' said Uncle Fanel with a sigh.

'Such gratitude,' replied Aunt Marian. 'When we've risked imprisonment to bring him this far.'

Uncle Fanel bent over Ion. 'You'll be all right,' he said. 'I promise. I left like you years and years ago, without a friend on the other side, and I've never regretted it. Are you frightened of the next frontier?'

Ion shook his head. 'It isn't that,' he said. 'It's leaving Grandma alone. What will happen to her?'

'She's in her own village.'

'She's too old to be left. I promised Grandpa that I would stay, that I would see her buried.'

Uncle Fanel rumpled his hair. 'You're too young to think about that sort of thing. Come on, back in the car. There'll be plenty of people to bury the old lady.'

'Have a sweet,' said Sandra.

'I liked the village,' exclaimed Marcus. 'I wouldn't leave it, not if I was in Ion's shoes. I liked fetching water from the pump, and it was lovely without any cars.'

'You don't know what you're saying,' replied Aunt Marian.

The frontier was nothing but a smudge on the horizon now. They were nearly out of the plains. Beyond lay woods and a town and further still, another frontier. Once Ion was across that frontier there would be no going back. It was the point of no return. He dreaded reaching it. His whole heart cried out, I want to go back.

They bought food in a town and lunched by a river. The peasants did not speak Ion's language any more.

'The day after tomorrow you will see the sea,' said Aunt Marian, speaking slowly and carefully. 'The sea.' He nodded. He tried to like her; but he failed. The sea, he thought, miles of water, a lake with salt in it. What is so special about that?

'No more buckets to carry, soon your arms will grow straight, your shoulders will unbend. You won't know yourself,' laughed Aunt Marian.

'No, they won't. They'll stay like that for ever,' cried Rosie.

'Yes, Ion. You'll always be different, you'll never fit in,' said Sandra.

'Shut up,' said Don. He hit Sandra and suddenly they were tumbling about by the river fighting each other, and Ion was running away, back along the road, his heart thudding against his

sides, sweat running down his face. He knew they would come after him. But at least he would have tried. He would not have deserted Grandma without trying to go back. Perhaps Grandpa was looking down from heaven watching him, crying, 'Run faster, don't let them catch you.' For now he felt as though he had wings, as though nothing could hold him back. He kicked off the English sandals as he ran. The road was hot, but the soles of his feet were thick. He could hear voices behind him. Rosie was screaming. Then he heard Don shout, 'I'll fetch him . . . .' And he screamed to himself without making a sound, 'Ion, faster, run faster!'

It was a long time before Don passed him. Then he stopped and stood looking at him.

'Come back,' he said at last. 'It's better that way, then you won't be thrown into prison without a trial like Uncle Lucian and Aunt Tantza. You will have nothing to fear. If you go back you will always be frightened.'

Ion shook his head. 'I shall be all right,' he said in English.

Uncle Fanel stopped the car beside them then. 'Get in,' he shouted. 'At once.'

Ion climbed in like a beaten dog. 'You are a fool,' shouted Uncle Fanel. 'An imbecile. Why do you want to stay in your backward country? You owe it nothing. It has even taken your parents from you. And you want to go back, to the squalor and the inconvenience of it all. Who has ever heard of your village? No one. But everyone has heard of England, mention London and you'll see . . . .'

The tears were coming now, the tears he had held back all day.

'I want to make it great,' he shouted through his tears. 'I want to change things, to empty the prisons, to make just laws. I want to be a Minister. If I go, I'm running away. I'm not making anything any better. England was awful once, but people changed it.'

'Your country will never change,' said Uncle Fanel. 'People are too lazy and too ignorant.'

'That's not true,' shouted Ion. 'Everyone goes to school now, everyone. We learn French, not just the rich, all of us. I shall go to college.'

'Shut up,' shouted Uncle Fanel. 'I don't want to hear any more nonsense. I've heard enough.'

He was so angry that the veins stood out on his face. 'Get in the car, everyone,' he shouted. 'And no more talking. I know your country, Ion,' he continued. 'I grew up there. I know it better than you do.'

'You don't,' shouted Ion. 'You don't know how it is now. Things are getting better all the time. We have electricity in the village now, and a friend of mine has television, and there's a man in the village with a car. Soon they will asphalt the road.'

'Be quiet, or I will hit you. I can't drive with such nonsense in my ears,' shouted Uncle Fanel, and at last Ion understood. Uncle Fanel did not want to know, he did not want to understand for fear he might regret leaving all those years ago. Revisiting the village must have made him realise how lovely it was. In England there were no fresh chickens to eat, no ground maize, no plum brandy; no corn on the cob, as orange as a setting sun. There were cars, yes, but no slow moving oxen, no peace, no grapes to be gathered by the basketful, no long endless summer with tomatoes the size of tennis balls and the sounds of dogs barking in the night, and the cockerels heralding the dawn. You could not walk barefoot in England, nor be dirty-faced, nor sit on a hill and make a basket, nor spend a whole afternoon carving out a wooden spoon. He was sorry for Uncle Fanel now. But he did not mean to make the same mistake; at the first opportunity he was going back.

They were travelling faster now. It was as though Uncle Fanel's fury was helping to turn the wheels of the car. Once they nearly hit a cart loaded with maize. The English children were quiet. Uncle Fanel insisted that the car windows remained closed, so that the sweat ran off their faces, and their bare thighs stuck to the car seat.

Then at last, Uncle Fanel spoke and it was as though his mind had been listening in to Ion's mind, for this is what he said: 'I have no regrets about leaving, Ion. I want you to know that. I love England. It has given me everything I have - my car, my wife and children, my house, and more than that, a sense of freedom. That is why I want you to come with us. I want you to have the same good fortune. Do you understand what I am trying to tell you?'

'Yes, that you have no regrets. But you left a brother behind. I am leaving no one but Grandma.'

'All the better,' replied Uncle Fanel. 'Let no one else rot in their filthy prisons.'

'What is he saying?' shouted Marcus. 'Tell us, Daddy, translate.'

'Perhaps he should go back,' suggested Aunt Marian without regret. 'Perhaps we've made a mistake.'

'Go back?' shouted Uncle Fanel. 'How can he go back? And to what? When my mother dies who will look after him, I ask you? As if I haven't lain tossing and turning every night over the problem. Oh, the sleepless nights I've had worrying over Ion, you've no idea!'

'He doesn't want to come with us,' said Don, talking in English like his parents. 'You can see it on his face.'

'I'm not going through that frontier again,' shouted Marcus. 'I don't like the soldiers.'

Rosie began to cry. Sandra started to shout, 'I'm being squashed. I haven't any room. Tell Don to move. I can't breathe.'

There seemed no air anywhere, only the endless heat and the woods never seeming any nearer and the weight on Ion's heart which grew heavier each passing mile. He thought that it would be cooler walking with the cows, a long stick over his shoulder, his feet bare in the warm dust. What was Grandma doing now? he wondered. He had lost all sense of time. Most likely the cows would be inside and she would be sitting nodding on the verandah, her hands folded in her lap.

At last they reached the woods. 'We'll stop here and rest,' said Uncle Fanel, wiping sweat from his face. 'It's not more than fifty miles to the next border now.'

Ion walked into the wood and knelt by a tree. He had never prayed before, never in his whole life, for prayers were not allowed at school and his grandmother had not wished to force her faith upon him. But he prayed just the same for someone to tell him right from wrong. Should he go back for his grandmother's sake and imperil the lives of Uncle Fanel and his children? Or should he go on and forget his homeland for ever, the fields so rich and golden in the summer, so white and pure with snow in the winter? He waited for an answer, but none came. He walked back to the Camper, his head in his hands, and his answer was there on the road. An old woman was staggering under the weight of two wooden buckets; every few metres she stopped to rest; her back was bent by the weight, so far bent that it was impossible for her to look up. Her fingers

were as gnarled as the branches of a dead tree. She could have been his grandmother a few years hence. She wore the same kind of long black dress, shawl and kerchief, and her feet were bare. She muttered to herself and she walked so slowly that it seemed impossible that she should ever reach her destination.

'Let me carry them for you,' cried Ion holding out a hand. But she did not speak his language. She muttered something and shuffled on.

'She should be in a home for old people,' said

Aunt Marian. 'One day she will fall and never get up, like an old horse.'

Ion was waiting for a chance to go back now. It was too far to walk, he knew that, but now as though in answer to a prayer, he saw that there was a container van from his own country drawn up at the side of the road.

Uncle Fanel can look after his family and himself, he thought. Grandma matters more than the spoilt English children who always have their own way in everything, who cannot be rebuked without bursting into tears. It is my country and Grandma that matter. The others will survive. The driver of the van was just starting the engine when Ion reached it.

'Are you going to the frontier?' Ion asked. 'I crossed by mistake. I fell asleep.'

'Hop in,' replied the driver, speaking his own language. 'Though how you got across the frontier asleep beats me. The way they search my van sometimes, they don't miss a fly. Slam the door.' Ion opened the window to wave to the English children. 'Me go back,' he shouted in English. 'Goodbye.'

He saw only fury on Uncle Fanel's face and heard Marcus shout, 'Good luck.' What else they said was drowned by the roar of the engine as the driver swung the big container van onto the road and Ion saw a lizard running for its life, and that Rosie was crying again, and that the sun had disappeared at last behind the woods.

7
A Night Alone

The driver was small with the broad shoulders of an ox. His sleeves were rolled up, the front of his shirt was open, showing his broad hairy chest. He had short dark hair and a mouth which turned up at the corners as though he was for ever laughing, as though life to him was one long joke.

'So you want a lift back to the border, eh? You weren't running away, were you, sonny?' he asked laughing. 'I don't want any trouble.'

'I didn't mean to cross,' replied Ion quickly. 'And I've got to get back to help my grandma. She's very, very old, too old to manage on her own.'

He realised now that he had left all his luggage in Uncle Fanel's car, including the photograph and the locket with his mother's hair inside, so he would never see them again. The thought made him want to cry.

'You live with your grandma then?' asked the man.

Ion nodded. He felt very high up in the van. What was Uncle Fanel doing now? he wondered. Was he in pursuit? He could see nothing but an empty road behind. What were they all saying? Had they left the forest yet? Marcus would be on his side. Don would understand. But what about the others? Would they ever forgive him?

'You're a bit young to be travelling on your own,' said the driver.

'I was showing the tourists the way,' he said, and wondered where he had learned to lie.

'They should have woken you up at the border,' said the driver, his face crinkled with mirth. He took a cigarette out of a packet and lit it. 'It's all right, sonny. I don't want to know your business. If I had the chance to get out I would. But that's me. I haven't got a grandma to look after. Don't listen to me.' He started to sing while the van rumbled on through the hot countryside. Ion leaned back. Maybe he was a fool. Maybe he should have gone on. If only he had had a father to ask. Someone he could trust. But since Grandpa had died there was no one. The village was full of spies. If he had told someone they could have reported him to the police, just out of jealousy, though most got found out anyway. But you had to be careful. He had done his best. He was going back. When Grandma died he would be alone, but he might be a man by then. He was very tired. The day seemed to have started a week ago. But he wasn't going to cry, not in front of the driver. He had to get through the frontier without incriminating Uncle Fanel. It was not going to be easy. He thought of the watch towers with their guns protruding, of the armed soldiers, and of the raked no-man's land. People had tried before to get across and died on the barbed wire or breathed their last breath on the first piece of earth across the border. He was frightened now, too frightened to speak. He did not want to die yet. He was not ready. But was anybody ever ready? Would his parents be in heaven if he went there? In spite of the heat he felt cold, the sort of cold which reaches down to the marrow of your bones, which makes you shiver and sweat at the same time.

'You all right?' asked the driver presently.

'Yes, sure,' Ion answered. 'I'm looking forward to getting home.'

'*If* you get across the border,' replied the driver. 'I'm not looking for trouble.'

'I shall get out before we get there,' Ion replied. 'Just drop me off a mile or so away. I'll be all right.'

'I wish I could take you across. But I can't risk prison.'

'I've got some relations by the border. I will stop the night with them.'

'That's all right then.' The driver gave a sigh of

relief and lit another cigarette. 'You stop the night with them. They'll advise you, get you the right papers, explain everything. You'll be all right then.' It was as though he was trying to convince himself that Ion really would be all right.

'Do you like driving this van?' asked Ion.

'Oh yes, it's a grand life. I go across the border and I can buy coffee and nylon tights, presents for everyone.'

'Is it so good in the West?'

'It's fantastic. I'd stay if I got the chance. But I've got parents you understand. If I stayed across they would be arrested.'

'Yes, of course.'

Would Grandma have been arrested if he had gone to England? He had never thought of that! Perhaps she had been arrested already and marched away by the soldiers. Supposing there was no one at home when he returned? The whole village might be surrounded. 'One of my mates stayed over the other side, and they took his father. That was a few years ago of course,' said the driver.

Anything could have happened. He was trembling now.

'Anything wrong?' asked the driver.

Ion shook his head. 'Would they arrest an old lady?' he asked.

'Shouldn't think so. Here, have something to drink. I've got a thermos of coffee.'

The drink calmed Ion's nerves. And presently, miraculously, he slept, with his head on the driver's shoulder, and dreamed he was driving the geese through waist-high grass with Rosie riding on his shoulders.

It was dusk when he wakened and the driver was shaking him.

'We're eight kilometres from the border,' he said. 'Where do your relations live?'

For a moment Ion could not remember where he was, nor the time of day.

'Your relations, where do they live?' The man was shaking him again. He smelt of beer and tobacco. Bristles had grown on his chin. He needed a shave. His hands were covered with dark hair. Ion noticed all of this as though for the first time, and rubbed his eyes.

'Over there,' he said pointing to a farmstead. 'Drop me here. I'll be all right.'

'Lucky I stopped here,' said the man. 'Don't you have any luggage?' Ion shook his head. He jumped down from the cab. Geese were going home along the road, driven by a small boy. 'Good luck at the border,' said the man starting the van. 'Go straight to your relations. Don't

hang about.'

Ion waved. He felt very alone, more alone than he had ever felt before. There was a peculiar ache inside himself and his legs trembled when he walked. He had no money, no food and night was closing down over a land which was not his, whose language he could not speak.

Uncle Fanel will be across the second border by now, he thought. He will have used the other passport, the one I'm not on. He's a clever man. He thinks of everything. He will be saying to his family, what a fool Ion is! How could the boy be so stupid? And they will laugh and Aunt Marian will say, 'His arms aren't straight enough for England. He is nothing but a peasant boy.' But that's not true, Ion thought. Once we had a pair of horses and a carriage. Grandpa told me. We owned half the village then. The peasants worked the land in exchange for half of what they grew. The other half was ours. We were as wealthy as the English then. He carried his English sandals, for he found it easier to walk barefoot. Few cars approached the border. It was like walking along a road which ended at a wall, at nowhere. What if I cannot get across, what then? Prison? he thought. All of a sudden Ion was very tired. The tiredness swept over him like a wave dulling his senses. And now he simply put one foot in front of the other as darkness grew and now nothing mattered very much, not even the sharp pangs of hunger in his stomach. He reached a spring at last where goats were watered. There was a cup there and he drank from the goats' trough and washed the dust from his face. He could see very little now but in the distance a bell tolled. A funeral, he thought, so here some people still believe in God. If I had stayed with Uncle Fanel I might be safe now. I would be in a soft bed in a big house with a bathroom full of beautiful towels and sweet-smelling soap. I would have eaten strange food, Western food. There would be music playing - pop music. Suddenly Ion was full of regret. The road home seemed unbearably long and fraught with danger and difficulties. And his grandmother might have died in his absence and the villagers would laugh at him coming back. 'What a fool to miss such a chance!' they'd say.

Tears were running down Ion's cheeks now. The day seemed to have lasted for ever. And he had not even the photograph of his parents to look at now. He had lost all his belongings. He had only what he wore and they were strange English clothes. He started to walk on along the wide straight road which led only to the border, to the soldiers and no-man's land, to the entrance to his own land which was like a prison, which you could neither enter nor leave without special permission from the very government itself. When I'm a Minister that will be one of the first things

I'll change, he thought. People will come and go as they please. The frontiers will be open to everyone. I'll have the watch towers pulled down. But now Ion could hear a dog howling and he remembered his uncle telling him that the frontier was patrolled by soldiers with fierce dogs at night. And in the distance he could see the great arc of the searchlights scanning the ploughed fields for people trying to get across; and he began to tremble, and he thought, I don't want to try tonight, not tonight. Then a car came racing past full of laughing soldiers who shouted something out of the windows which he could not understand. And he remembered that this was considered an even crueller country than his own. I will try tomorrow, he thought, tomorrow I will feel stronger. I'm too tired tonight. He looked around and saw the outline of a shed across a patch of stubble land. When he reached it he found it empty and crawled inside and lay down on the dry earth inside. I will be brave in the morning, he thought. And by the evening with luck I'll be back in my own village relating my adventures. But no one will believe about the splendid hotel where we stayed. He curled up like a dog, because now he could not stop shivering. In the distance a cow lowed and he heard a train hooting like something possessed. Grandma will be pleased, he thought. She won't be alone any more. I shall look after her as I promised, and perhaps one day when I'm older I shall get another chance to go again to England. If my parents were alive this would never have happened, he thought next. We would be richer and Uncle Fanel would not have wanted to adopt me. My father might have been a Minister. He might have made things better. Probably they were shot, he thought a moment later. The soldiers took them out and shot them. How can I change anything? he thought desperately, when there are so many soldiers. When they can just take people from their homes in the night and never bring them back. And now without warning, dawn was coming, an early foreign dawn, with the sun rising all new and bright and the cocks crowing and the birds singing as though their lives depended on it.

I've been awake all night, thought Ion desperately. The stubble was veiled by a dewy mist and he could see rabbits on it nibbling quickly before daylight came. He rubbed his eyes. He wished that the day had passed already. That he could skip it altogether like one can skip pages in a book, and so find himself on the last piece of road between him and home. In the distance the searchlights went out. Fresh soldiers sped along the road. Tired soldiers came back. The same thing would be happening on the other side, his side. Would he ever see it again? He wandered down to the spring and washed his face and hands. In the early morning light he could see the border quite clearly, the place where the ground changed colour, the distant watch towers, the trench in which people fell when they were shot. I shall never get back, he thought, but I must try. I can't come so far without trying. I shall never see the underground trains now, decided Ion, walking towards the border, nor Buckingham Palace where the Queen of England lives. But if I become a Minister I might be sent there - who knows? And then the Queen might ask me to dinner. And suddenly in the bright sunlight of early morning with the air fresh and full of hope, anything seemed possible.

8
'I Want the Truth'

Ion had reached the border. He stood behind a long line of lorries. His own country lay beyond. He could see wooded hills, the dim outline of mountains, acres of yellow stubble, one-storey houses built out of mud bricks; the long straight road to home. He felt like a moth beating against a window trying to get into a lighted room. The ploughed land was being raked by a slow-moving peasant. The soldiers were in their watch towers. They looked harmless enough, but were certainly ready to kill. He looked at the lorries and knew that they were his only hope. If only he could get inside one and conceal himself. But most of them were State-owned container lorries. There was no way of getting inside them and no room underneath to hide either. There were hardly any cars yet. It was too early for visitors with the dew still wet on the grass. He sat down on the verge and waited. The drivers chatted and smoked, waiting their turn. He could hear laughter coming from the soldiers. Supposing they were the same ones as were there yesterday? Supposing they recognised him?

The lorries moved on, leaving him alone on the verge. The grass was blackened by petrol fumes and diesel oil. Only a hundred metres away a small girl was watching a flock of geese. What would they do if they caught him? The thought made him tremble. He must not think of it. He would not be caught. There was a lorry parked near him now full of sacks. He could climb inside and hide. The driver had disappeared in the direction of the frontier, leaving the engine running. For a moment Ion's legs refused to move. Then he bounded across the road and clambered into the lorry. The sacks were empty and smelt of maize. He pulled some over his head and lay down, afraid to breathe. Presently the driver came back laughing. They were all like that, Ion decided, always laughing because they felt so important driving their big trucks, passing the slow-moving oxen, nearly running down old ladies, hooting loudly all the time, frightening horses, leaving a trail of petrol fumes behind them. The lorry was moving now. Ion curled up tightly, his fists clenched so that the white of the knuckles showed. He felt the lorry stop again. Obviously they were through the first barrier, but still on the wrong side. The soldiers were quick. They laughed and made cheerful remarks and then the lorry moved on and now the soldiers spoke

Ion's language.

'What have you got inside?' they asked letting down the tailboard. 'How long have you been away?'

Ion held his breath until he felt he would burst.

'Why don't you fold the sacks neatly? Anything could hide under that heap,' asked a soldier.

Ion heard him scrambling into the lorry.

'What should I want to bring in?' asked the driver. 'I'm a poor man.'

'Spies from the West. Records . . . anything . . . .' He touched Ion's legs. 'And there *is* something here,' he said. 'I was right. I have a feeling for such things. As soon as I saw this truck I knew it contained contraband goods.'

'A boy!'

'The driver knew nothing about me. It is not his fault, please, sir,' said Ion.

'You had better come inside,' said the soldier. 'You too, driver.'

'I didn't know. I swear to God I didn't know,' replied the driver, who was a thin man with very little hair and high cheek bones, a man who looked as though he had worked himself to a shadow. Ion was sorry for him. Perhaps he had a family waiting for him at home. The soldiers might shoot him. And it is all my fault, thought Ion.

'You come from our country,' said the soldier with a cap. 'Sit down. What were you doing on the other side?'

Ion was silent for a moment. He knew he must be very careful. He was sitting in an office now, facing an officer who had a moustache and strong hands and didn't smile, though his mouth was full of teeth.

'I crossed by mistake yesterday. I had a lift in a cart pulled by oxen. I fell asleep.'

The officer consulted a list. 'No cart pulled by oxen crossed yesterday,' he said.

'It wasn't here. It was somewhere else. It wasn't a big crossing. I woke up and got out and found myself lost,' said Ion desperately. 'Truly, sir.'

'Get on the phone and check up. Find out if any oxen pulling a wagon crossed anywhere.' A girl in uniform picked up a telephone receiver. She was quite young and very pretty. Ion would have liked her for a sister.

'You slept then?' said the officer.

Ion nodded. Another man was questioning the driver, who had not been allowed to sit down. There were beads of sweat on the driver's face. He kept repeating, 'I had no idea.'

'Your name, please,' asked the soldier. 'And your address.'

Ion gave his real name and the name of his village.

'Check that,' the officer told the girl. 'See if it exists. And get on to headquarters.'

Ion wondered when they would start to torture him. Nothing would make him tell them about Uncle Fanel. He would stick to his first story. He would not change a single word. He was trembling now. The girl talked to the officer in a low voice. Then she fetched him some biscuits and a cup of coffee. Ion could not look at the biscuits. They made him want to cry.

The lorry driver was still standing. It was very hot in the building. A queue of cars waited outside. The officer nibbled a biscuit.

'How are your relations from England? Did they enjoy their stay with you?' he asked presently. 'Are you sorry they have gone with their four beautiful children?'

'Yes, sir. I liked them a lot. They were very cheerful and loved our beautiful land.'

'You must have crossed with them yesterday, but how?' asked the officer, passing him a biscuit.

'I wandered across. Really. I got in the boot when they weren't looking. They were very, very angry, sir.'

'And threw you out?'

'They told me to go back.'

'If they had been civilised they would have brought you back and explained everything.'

'They were in a hurry.'

'First the oxen, then the boot. When are you going to tell the truth?'

In a minute he will torture me, thought Ion. Please, God, help me. Tell me what to say. Someone help me. Grandpa, if you're in heaven, tell me. Mother, please speak now. The biscuit had turned to sawdust in his mouth.

'It is all lies,' said the officer wearily. 'If you were escaping to the West, why did you come back?'

'I wasn't. I'm returning home to look after my grandmother. She's very old. I just wanted a ride to the border. I wanted to see what was on the other side.'

'I want the truth,' shouted the officer, banging the table so hard that the coffee jumped out of his cup.

Ion's hands started to shake.

'They were trying to get you out? Admit it.'

'No.'

'You're doing no good,' said the girl. 'You are only frightening the boy. Let me talk to him. He will tell me everything.'

She beckoned to Ion. 'Come and have a wash and some coffee. I have a brother the image of you.'

The driver had disappeared, but his lorry was still parked outside. Ion followed the girl into a room at the back of the building. She fetched him towels and soap. She had fair hair and soft brown eyes. 'I want to help you,' she said. 'You will let me, won't you?'

He didn't want to say anything. He liked her;

he wanted to go on liking her. But was she really on his side? He washed and drank the cup of coffee she brought him and ate a sugared bun, and with it strength came back.

'Better?' asked the girl smiling. 'Now tell me everything.'

'I have. I came here with my English cousins and crossed without them knowing and came back today to return to my grandmother. There is nothing else to say.'

The girl talked sweetly to him, she patted his hand and fetched him another sugar bun and told him that he was a very handsome little boy and

that she liked his chic English shirt, which must have come from Marks and Spencer, where the English bought all their clothes. She felt the texture of it and looked at the sandals and the shiny English jeans which were spattered with diesel oil. 'Where is your mother?' she asked presently.

'The soldiers killed her.'

'And your father too?'

He nodded.

'That is bad,' she said. 'Now you tell the truth or you will end the same way,' and she started to shout at him and bang the table as the officer had done.

'Just the truth, all we want is the truth. You got across the border without being seen. How?'

'In the boot,' said Ion beginning to cry. 'You were here, but you did not see. You were all here.'

'I was not here yesterday. It was my day off.'

'There was a girl anyway,' he said.

'You want to be shot?'

'I don't mind,' said Ion. 'I only mind for my grandma who needs me. I don't mind for myself.' And the English in their Camper seemed to belong to another world. They could cross frontiers as they pleased. They were free. But as for himself he could not even get back into his own particular prison. He put his head in his hands. Let them shoot me, he thought. It is my own fault for coming back.

When he looked up the girl had gone. A young soldier shook him by the shoulder. 'It's all right,' he said. 'You can go home.'

'Go home?'

'Yes. Go back to your grandmother. Have you any luggage? I'll take you to the nearest town and give you some money. You can catch a train. Have you ever travelled by train?'

Ion shook his head.

'Don't worry. You'll be all right. I expect your relations wanted you and why not? You are an orphan after all. We don't want any scandal here. You just go home and say nothing, eh?'

Ion nodded.

'That will be the best way for all of us. Let me carry you. You must be very tired,' said the soldier. 'I have a very nice car. You will enjoy the journey.'

Ion wondered where he was really going. Was the soldier speaking the truth or was he being taken somewhere to be tortured or shot, quietly and happily so that the tourists waiting outside would not be upset?

'I can walk,' he said. 'But not with shoes, because my feet are covered with blisters.'

9
A Journey with a Soldier

Ion climbed into the back of the khaki-coloured military car. He felt very nervous. He sat on the edge of the seat with his fists clenched. It was another hot day. There were thirty or more tourists hanging about in summer dresses, shorts, linen trousers. Their faces were burned by the sun already. There was a Camper and a very large American car, and lots of children dressed in western clothes. Ion looked at them and wondered whether he was mad to be here in a car waiting to be tortured when he might have been across the border. The soldier had creases at the back of his neck. His hair was short under his cap. The barrier was lifted for him without any to-do. Other soldiers saluted him. Obviously he was important.

He had a bag of sweets in his pocket. 'Have one?' he offered turning round in his seat. 'Take two and relax, no one is going to hurt you. All that is ended.' Ion read no significance into his words. As far as he was concerned they were probably lies. He leaned back on his seat and sucked the two sweets one after another. The roads were almost empty and the soldier drove very fast, hooting impatiently at the few old people and oxen which they met.

'You like the car, eh?' he enquired and Ion merely nodded, not wishing to make a friend of him, suspecting him of all sorts of unspeakable crimes.

'So you've never been on a train before?'

'No. We have our own two cows,' replied Ion as though that explained everything.

'Of course,' replied the soldier smiling to himself. 'And you milk the cows? I come from such a village myself.'

'I shall leave it when I'm older. I intend to be a Minister.'

'Bravo,' shouted the soldier laughing.

And then suddenly Ion was overcome by sleep. Against his will his eyes closed and the car rocked him as he had been rocked in his cradle years and years ago. He thought, if I'm tortured, I'm tortured. There's nothing more I can do. I've done my best. And dimly as though from a distance, he heard the soldier turn on the car radio before he slept.

They were in a town. It was market day. There were stalls of fruit everywhere; chickens tied together by their legs, white ducks with yellow bills protruding from sacks. They would all have made Sandra cry, recollected Ion. The soldier was shaking him awake. He handed him two meat balls wrapped in paper. 'Eat. Then you will feel better,' he said.

Everything came back to Ion then. The shouting officer, the girl, the car journey. He wanted to run, but he saw the soldier had a gun in his belt. He'll shoot me down, thought Ion. I'll lie among the stalls with the poor quaking ducks and die. He took the meat balls.

'Where's the station?' he asked. 'I thought we were going to a station.'

The soldier smelt of beer. 'Only another ten kilometres,' he replied laughing. 'I'll put you on the train.'

He stood staring at the girls walking along the pavement. 'What legs!' he exclaimed. 'But you are too young to appreciate them, eh?'

Ion nodded slowly. 'I don't intend to marry. I am going to work very hard and become someone important. That is if I live long enough,' he added quickly.

The soldier looked at his watch. 'We must go on,' he said. 'We must not miss your train.'

'What sort will it be?' asked Ion.

'A big one, a beauty.' He offered him sweets. The car was too hot to touch. The ducks' bills were open and the chickens gasped pathetically. They swept out of the town, hooting at everything which dared to put a foot on the road. The soldier started to sing. Uncle Fanel will be driving towards England now. He will be halfway home, thought Ion.

The station was full of people. The soldier parked in the front ignoring the *No Parking* signs. There was an old lady carrying a goose in a sack, and women in high-heeled shoes and men carrying cases, or hampers full of food. Someone had dropped a bottle and wine was running down the street in a red trickle like blood.

'Stay near me,' said the soldier. 'I'll get your tickets. I have eyes in the back of my head so don't run off anywhere.'

He could have been across the border by now and here he was at the station going home. But was he really going home? Or was it some trick to get him somewhere? Did they still intend to torture him? How could he tell? He wanted to run, but he was too frightened; besides there was still a chance that the soldier was honest, that he was really going back to his village and he did not want to risk death yet, not until he saw his torturers and knew there was no more hope.

'Come on, your train is in,' said the soldier.

People looked at them as they hurried across

the station. The train waited, puffing out steam. Half the carriages were full.

'I remember my first journey by train,' said the soldier smiling. 'We had a hamper full of chicken and rolls and wine, and ripe tomatoes just picked. What a journey it was! Father drank too much and kept bursting into song, and it was snowing outside.'

He opened a carriage door. There was a middle-aged lady inside holding the hand of a little girl. The soldier took off his hat.

'Madam,' he said, 'could you be so kind as to keep an eye on this boy until he reaches Augusta? He is on his own.'

'Yes, of course.' Ion looked at the lady. She wore a hat and had dark hair drawn back from her face and brown eyes. He stepped up into the carriage. He did not intend to thank the soldier, who handed him more sweets and said, 'Good journey and the best of luck.'

'What a nice man,' said the lady as the soldier shut the door. 'Is he your father?'

Ion shook his head. He did not intend to speak to her either, for she could have been planted there for the soldier's benefit and she might start questioning him. Ion stood in the corridor watching the soldier leaving the station. He walked swiftly, smiling at people. Ion wished that it was possible to like him.

The train was starting now. The waving people on the platform slid from view. Waving travellers left the corridor to find their seats. Soon he was alone in the corridor staring at the countryside. The train was running alongside a wide river. The sky was an endless, cloudless blue. In spite of himself Ion was suddenly happy, for it was impossible to be sad when he was travelling on a real train for the first time. There were ships on the river, and laughing children swimming and people picnicking alongside the slow-running water. I shall be able to tell Grandma about it, he thought, about everything.

'Come inside,' said the lady opening the carriage door. 'Have a bon-bon.'

'No thank you, I would rather stay here.'

Perhaps he really was going home. How surprised the village would be to see him back again! If only Grandma was still alive. In two weeks it would be time to start school. He was going to work hard, harder than he had ever worked before. He had to if he was going to be a Minister. They had left the river now. The train raced through a long tunnel. Smuts flew into his eyes through the open window. Lights came on in carriages. He would have to walk from Augusta. It was five miles along a hot, dusty road. What time would the train reach the station? Would the cows be pleased to see him? The young one might have had a calf. He wished he still had the photograph of his parents. His mother was very beautiful, more beautiful than the lady in the carriage. But he could not remember, not one single thing about her. The train was entering a station now.

'This is not where you get out,' said the lady opening the carriage door. The little girl had fallen asleep. Ion suddenly envied her. He wished that he had someone to travel about the world with, someone who loved him.

'I know,' he answered.

The platform was crowded. More and more people pushed their way onto the train; some of them were singing. There were soldiers too walking about with machine guns. For a terrifying moment Ion thought that they were looking for him. He rushed into the carriage and sat down by the lady. 'There are lots of soldiers outside with guns,' he said.

'Don't worry. They are not looking for you,' she replied patting his hand and laughing. 'Why should they be after you? You have gone quite pale. You are a funny little boy.'

'I'm ten,' said Ion. 'And that isn't little.'

He went back to the corridor, which was crowded with people and cases. Two men were drinking out of beer bottles and singing. The hottest part of the day was over. The train slid out of the station, leaving the soldiers behind still standing with their machine guns. Perhaps there were always soldiers with guns in stations. Ion did not know, never having been on a train before. One of the men drinking beer slapped Ion on the shoulder.

'We're free now,' he cried.

'Free?' asked Ion. 'Have you just come out of prison?'

'Prison! And why should I have been in prison?' glowered the man.

'He's quite drunk,' said someone else. 'I should return to your carriage.'

They were by the river again and on the other side lay mountains majestically raising tree-covered slopes to the evening sky.

'Only another hour,' said the lady looking at a wrist watch. 'I expect you will be glad to be home again. Your mummy must be anxious about your returning. Have you been visiting relations?'

'I went to see some friends off,' Ion answered staring out of the window, 'and got lost. Anyway I haven't got a mother. I live with my grandma.'

He recognised the hills in the distance now. He was riding on a train he had seen in the distance so often as nothing but a plume of smoke in the sky; a few more minutes and his own valley would come into view. But first another stop. There were crowds on the platform. Passengers were welcomed with kisses. There was the smell of the country outside, of cow dung and ripe grapes and the simple, uncomplicated smells of earth and maize and sour wine.

It was as though Ion could smell his own village already.

'Don't get out yet,' called the lady.

'I'm only looking,' replied Ion.

He felt nervous now. Would they welcome him home? Or would people stand and laugh at him, crying, 'What a fool to come back! We would have looked after your grandmother.'

And what would she say? How would she greet him? If only she would be pleased. If only she would cry, 'I've missed you so. I've mourned your departure every hour of the day and night. Thank God you have returned.' Then he would be happy. Too happy for words.

10
'She's Dead, isn't She?'

'Here we are!'

The lady stepped down first. Ion helped the little girl. The station was a small one with two platforms and the road just outside running straight and beautiful in the evening light.

'Goodbye then. You know the way home, don't you? Give your ticket to the ticket collector.' She held out a gloved hand. Ion shook it and walked out of the station and away along the tree-lined road to home. A succession of cement lorries passed him covering him with grey dust. A small girl watched cows grazing the grass verge. It was a lovely evening, clear and sunlit with the peace of an ending summer. Ion swung his arms, which Aunt Marian had found so peculiar. He could not stop himself whistling, for soon he would be among his own people again, in his own village. Life would return to normal, the spring would come again, another spring, another harvest, another gathering of the grapes. Every few minutes he ran a few metres, and presently he could see the trees which stood along the ridge above his village. It will be raining in England, he thought, and the underground trains will be full of people pushing and gasping for air. And I would have had to wear shoes all the time and walk with my arms straight. I would not have fitted in, he thought, and the little girls would have called me 'crooked arms'. All the same as he walked a sadness stole over him for the opportunity he had missed, which would never come again.

He took the short-cut home, past the well which had his grandfather's name carved on it along with several others. (They had paid for it to be sunk and their names would be there for ever.) Past the young willows, the branches of which he had cut to make baskets, past the blackberry bushes heavy with blackberries, round by the church where dogs ran at him barking and snarling. He stoned them mercilessly, thinking, Sandra would call me cruel, but she will never understand that they are not English dogs, not pets, but dogs kept as guards, fierce dogs who sometimes have rabies. There was a pig tethered in the churchyard by the priests' graves; for no one but priests was ever buried in the churchyard nor ever had been. He was nearly home now and his heart started to beat against his ribs like a hammer, and his blood seemed to run faster through his veins. He could not stop himself hurrying. He had to see whether Grandma was all right, that she had survived without him. He felt as though he had been away for years. He started to run. He wanted to shout, 'Grandma, I'm home. I've come back.'

But then he saw that there was a crowd gathered outside the house and that the yard gates were open. Half the village seemed to be there, and there could only be one reason for that - Grandma was dead. He dropped into a walk. Tears began to cascade down his small dirty face. He had come back to follow her to the hill to be buried, nothing more. Now he would live alone in the house. And how would he manage with the cows and the geese and the harvest to be seen to as well as school? He would never make a government Minister now. He would never alter anything. He should have gone with Uncle Fanel. He would have given him everything - a new bike, new clothes. His arms would have straightened with time and Sandra would have stopped insulting him. But no, he had to come back! He despised himself utterly standing there with the sweat and the tears mixing with the dirt on his face. And then he heard someone cry, 'Ion! It's Ion. Come at once! Don't stand there. Come.' And he said, 'She's dead, isn't she? I'm too late.'

The speaker was a peasant and she rushed forward and picked him up in her arms. She smelt of garlic and home-made soap, of cow and sun-baked earth. Her name was Nina and she had six cows and worked from dawn to dusk, because her husband Andre had lost a leg in some long forgotten war. He was there too, unshaven, with a bottle of red wine in his hand. She's dead, Ion thought again. She must be, but then why are they drinking? Everything looked the same, but slightly different too because he had been away and so was seeing it all as though for the first time. But Grandma was sitting in a chair looking older than she had when he had left, which was just a few days ago but now seemed like months. So she is not dead! That was Ion's first thought.

'She couldn't manage without you,' Nina said. 'We found her lying exhausted by the vineyard. It is a miracle that you have returned,' and she made the sign of the cross.

Grandma rose out of the chair with her arms outstretched. 'What made you come back? But you are so dirty and woebegone. Did they turn you back at the frontier?' she asked.

Nina had put him down. Others looked on through the open doorway. They were Ion's friends, his people, his life. But because he had been away, they all looked slightly different; even the carpets hanging on the walls were suddenly beautiful, for he had never really looked at them before, just accepted them as he had accepted everything.

Then Grandma said, 'The government has fallen, Ion. There is to be an amnesty.' And suddenly that explained everything - why he had been taken away from the frontier post, the soldiers at the station. So now everything would be different. And maybe one day he might be a Minister after all. Who could tell what the future might hold now?

A peasant was opening another bottle of wine. Soon he would be singing. Dark haired, brown eyed, he said, 'We must drink to Ion's return. But why did you come back? To go was the chance of a lifetime.'

Ion thought of the journey, of the long straight roads, of the hotel where they had stayed, of all that had happened. How could he tell anyone how he had felt when he hardly knew himself? So he smiled and said only, 'I had to know whether Grandma was all right.'

Then he looked round the small house with the familiar furniture and the same old pots and pans, and knew wherever he went it would always be home. Whatever I become, however important, I will always come back here, he thought. Even

when Grandma is gone it will still be my real home.

But now there was another noise - a hooting and a shouting which set all the dogs of the village barking and someone cried, 'It's Fanel back again. He must have returned for Ion.' And Ion thought, this is my second chance, but I'm not going. I'm not going to leave Grandma whatever anyone says. I don't want to be English, because this is my country. I don't need new shoes and I'm too old for toys, and in time I'll have a bike.

'Have you got Ion? We lost him across the border. I'm afraid he may be hurt or even arrested,' called Fanel anxiously.

'He's here, my son,' called Grandma. 'Don't stand outside. Come in, we're celebrating,' and she sounded different now, younger and full of hope.

'He returned to be with his grandma. Maybe he was homesick. Who knows?' asked Nina planting a kiss of welcome on Fanel's cheek.

Soon people moved outside to make room for Fanel and his family. More wine was poured. The dogs stopped barking. Ion could hear a cow lowing. And he wasn't sad that he hadn't gone to England, not any more.

Everyone was drinking to the new government now. Then some peasants linked arms and sang the National Anthem, the old forbidden one which had been abolished along with real freedom a long time ago.

'I've changed my mind. I'm not going to England, not till I can come back again,' Ion said quietly. 'I'm not like you Uncle Fanel. I'm sorry.'

'He was much older when he went,' Grandma said.

'Don't let's have a post mortem,' Aunt Marian exclaimed, and though Ion couldn't understand what she said, he thought, she's glad. She didn't really want me. I would never have smelt English, however often I washed. And I would never have been able to be myself. He could see it all now. He would have had to be someone else for ever and ever, like an actor. But best of all he had kept his promise to Grandpa. He would never leave Grandma again.

'I know how you feel, Ion, and I think you're right,' Don said suddenly.

'He wouldn't have fitted in. Is that what you mean?' Aunt Marian asked.

'Not exactly. What I mean is, here he is somebody. In England he would never have really been one of us, however hard we all tried. And now the government has fallen, everything may change here,' Don replied.

They were still singing the National Anthem

outside, still the old one, never the new one. It brought tears to Grandma's eyes.

'In your place, I wouldn't have left either, if that's any help, Ion,' Don said.

'People would have laughed at him,' Sandra added. 'And asked him why his arms were bent.'

'I think he's right to come back. It's lovely here,' Marcus said. Ion liked them now, more than ever before.

'You'll come back next year, won't you?' he asked in faltering English.

'Maybe,' replied Aunt Marian. 'But you've cost us a lot of trouble and a lot of money.'

'And umpteen problems,' added Uncle Fanel.

Then Ion told them how he had returned home. 'You don't understand, I was almost tortured and if it hadn't been for the government falling I wouldn't be here, now,' he finished in his own tongue. 'I could be dead or broken into pieces. Maybe a cripple for life.'

'Yes, you were very silly,' Uncle Fanel said. 'We might all have been imprisoned because of you. And now you will be here for ever. You'll never see the world.'

But Ion didn't mind, not any more. Uncle Fanel could say what he liked, he knew now that he had been right to come back.

Then Grandma spoke. She said, 'Now there's

an amnesty, your mother and father may return, Ion. We don't know for certain yet. But we can hope.' And he saw that there were tears splashing down her cheeks, tears of hope and joy.

People were setting up a table on the verandah now. They were bringing food and brightly coloured cloths. There were children marching up and down the earth road outside pretending to be soldiers. And an old man was fetching water. Gradually the little house was filled with people. Some poured wine, and they all talked about the amnesty, about who might come back and who was lost forever. To Ion it seemed like a dream, but a good dream, where things would come right in the end.

He saw his parents returning, the long table set up outside in the sunshine, the one only used for weddings and feast days, the special one. He saw them all dressed in their feast day clothes and a gipsy band playing. Then, in his mind, he heard the laughter and saw the raised glasses. He hardly knew his parents. But, if they returned, his mother would look after Grandma and the cows, and his father would soon be strong again, and able to chop the wood and fetch the water. I can go to college then, he thought. I can go to town and join the government and alter things and be really free and never be responsible for Grandma, nor the cows again. Then Vasile lifted him onto a chair, and Grandma raised her glass and cried, 'To Ion who found his way back across the frontier.'

And everyone cried, 'To Ion.'

It seemed the greatest moment of his life as he looked at their familiar faces, sunburnt with many lines and hardened by years of toil. Another minute and they were raising their glasses to Uncle Fanel and his family and Ion thought that was like life - things came and went, only the village stayed the same, and even that might not be for ever.